HIGH STAKES

WAYLAND
www.waylandbooks.co.uk

First published in 2013 by Wayland

Text copyright © Andrew Fusek Peters 2013
Illustration copyright © Cathy Brett 2013

Wayland
338 Euston Road
London NW1 3BH

Wayland Australia
Level 17/207 Kent Street
Sydney, NSW 2000

Series Editor: Louise John
Series design: Robert Walster
Design: Lisa Peacock
Consultant: Fiona Collins

A CIP catalogue record for this book is available
from the British Library.

ISBN 9780750268981

Printed in China

Wayland is a division of Hachette Children's Books,
an Hachette UK Company

www.hachette.co.uk

HIGH STAKES

Andrew Fusek Peters
and Cathy Brett

Titles in the series

The Crawling Hand

9780750268950

Sliced in Two

9780750268967

Wolf Boy

9780750268974

High Stakes

9780750268981

CHAPTER 1

Sam was crying. Which was odd because she never cries.

"Hey, what's up?" I didn't know whether to hug her or not.

"Nothing," she sniffed and tried to walk away.

We were outside on the school field. Break was nearly done and my best mate was far from happy.

"Sam! If you can't tell me, who can you tell?"

Sam looked up at me with her big green eyes. Something inside my chest went ping!

"Look, Jas. You might be the best detective I know, but there's nothing you can do this time. It's the new girl," she said.

"What, Vladya Blud-chik? Dead pretty, in a pale kind of way?"

"Yeah, thanks, Jas. That's really helpful."

"I'm a boy. Can't help it. What about her?"

"She's having a party Saturday night. All the girls are invited. She told them on facebook. But not me."

"Big deal. A bunch of crisps, some coke and too much gossip? No thanks."

"You're a boy. You don't understand." Sam sniffed again.

The bell saved me. "Cheer up! Let's talk later!"

Sam frowned and walked off. I
was walking down the corridor when
I saw her. Vladya Blud-chik. Since
when was it cool to wear sunglasses
indoors? She had bright red lipstick
and a smile that killed me dead.

10

One of Sam's mates looked over at me as if I was a piece of dirt. Vladya was talking and they were all hanging on to her every word. Her words sent shivers down my spine.

"In my country, yes, we have old ways of doing things. The old people hang garlic round their windowsills to ward off evil spirits. Hah! What do they know?"

Vladya's accent made my knees turned to jelly. Get a grip, Jas! I told myself. This is the girl who made your best mate cry!

CHAPTER 2

It was all over the news the next day. The old guy who had gone out for a walk and ended up dead. My mum was reading the paper.

"Says here, he dropped dead of a heart attack. Poor old man! Make us

some more toast, will you Jas?"

"Yeah, yeah."

While I waited for the toaster, I googled the man's death on my mobile. Don't ask me why. Some online geek had found out the man

was not only dead, but all his blood had vanished. As if something had sucked him dry. Shivers went down my spine. Again.

"I wouldn't want you dropping dead!" said Mum.

"Me neither," I muttered.

Mum was flinging butter on her toast and grabbing her coat. She blew me a kiss and slammed the door.

Five minutes later I was outside Sam's house.

"Morning!" I said.

"I suppose so." Sam was still in
a mood.

"That girl…" I started.

"You fancy her, don't you?" Sam
said angrily.

I tried to hide the blush.

"I can see the way you look at her.

Not that I care, right?"

"Course not. And I don't look at her in any way, I promise." In my heart of hearts I knew that Vladya would be trouble. "I've got my eyes on someone much closer to home…"

"Anyone I know?" A small smile

broke Sam's bad mood.

"Now that would be telling." I changed the subject. "Did you read about the guy who dropped dead?"

"In the park? Yeah."

"It's the bit about the blood that gets me…"

"What are you talking about?"

"The man had no blood in his body. What does that remind you of Sam?"

"Vampires? You must be kidding."

"I'm dead serious."

CHAPTER 3

"Bloody heck!" Sam cried.

"Yeah. Bloody alright."

"Vampires. Round here?"

"We've dealt with ghosts and werewolves. Are you surprised?"

"I guess not," Sam grinned.

"Me neither. And if it is vampires, then it's murder."

"Not if the old man wakes up again. You know, undead and all that. Turns into a vampire himself."

"A bit too late for that. He was cremated this morning, according to my phone."

At that moment, things got scary. We were walking down an alley, a shortcut to school. The sky was grey

as usual. With all the trees, the alley
was gloomy. A figure stepped out in
front of us.

"Good morning," said the figure.
Red lips. Pale skin. When she smiled,
I could see pointy teeth.

"Vladya!" said Sam. "What are you doing here?"

"I go to school this way. Nice to see you. Who is this boy?"

"I'm… J… Jas," I stuttered. I put out my hand. She shook it.

25

Her fingers were gentle to the touch, but ice-cold.

"We were just talking about the man who died last night," said Sam.

"Ah yes? So sad."

Sam stepped back and looked at

Vladya. "Yeah. Odd about all that blood. Vanished. Makes you think there might be some truth to tales about vampires!"

Vladya stepped closer. "You should not believe in such things!" she hissed. It felt like a threat.

But then a door banged and two boys ran out of one of the houses that led onto the alley. "Alright, Jas, Sam?" one of them shouted over.

Vladya strode off in a huff.

"Are you thinking what I'm thinking?" I said.

"Well, if she is," said Sam, "we can't really go to the police. 'Hey Officer, the man with the heart attack had his blood sucked by a vampire in year eight!'"

"When you put it like that, we're stuck," I grinned.

CHAPTER 4

"We have to stop her somehow," said Sam.

All day, we'd been staying away from the school fields, the canteen, anywhere she might be. "And your plan is?" I asked.

"Stick a sharp wooden stick through her heart!"

"Come on, Sam. I know the Facebook thing was bad, but really. Would you actually do it?"

"Don't know," she sighed.

"Anyhow, there's far too much at stake…" I smirked.

"Is that your idea of a joke?" Sam smiled.

"Yeah. Not bad, eh? Look, got some stuff to do, see you later."

I had to get onto the internet, fast, and see what I could find.

It was dark when we met up. I'd crept out hoping my parents wouldn't hear. "Are you sure this is the place?" I whispered.

"Yeah. I broke into the school office. This is her address alright."

The place was hardly spooky. A semi in a suburb, with all the lights off. An upstairs window was open.

"I reckon that's hers."

"Why?"

"Gut feeling. What now?"

"We lure her out."

"There is no need to do that!" a voice hissed. We both jumped. Vladya stepped out of the shadows right in front of us.

"Right. Thing is, we know all about you." I tried to keep calm.

"You do?" she replied.

"Yeah, leeches like you are all give and no take. Specially when it comes to blood!" said Sam.

"And now I shall have yours. Which of you shall I kill first, hmm?"

In the light, her teeth shone.

"Stay back, I'm armed!" I said, pulling a long packet from my coat.

Vladya laughed. "Garlic bread. That is so funny I could die laughing. Except I am dead already!" She came towards us. "And… in a minute, so will you be!"

CHAPTER 5

"Stop!" I shouted.

"But why? Will you throw some onions at me? Or stab me with a wooden stake?"

"No, but I do have back-up. You're surrounded," I said.

"Your lies are charming, but useless," smiled Vladya.

"Perhaps we should run?" Sam whispered.

"Nothing can outrun me!" Vladya towered over us, ready to grab our necks and bite us into eternity.

"Perhaps I can be of help?" The voice was posh and deep.

It came from a man who suddenly stood between us and living death.

"Harold?" Vladya squeaked.

"Yes, my dear. It seems you have been playing truant again."

"No. It was not me. I promise!" She shrank back into the shadows.

"Hey!" Sam nudged me. "He's

not alone…" And he wasn't. The shadows were full of figures. "Who are they all?"

"Friends. Believe it or not. Same as Vladya," said Harold.

"Oh, no!" Sam cried. "We're going to be blood sandwiches!"

"Don't worry, young girl. Such things are now against our law. That's what bloodbanks are for!" the

old vampire explained. "This girl is an outcast. She will now be punished. The olders are waiting for her..."

"Noooo!" Vladya screamed as she was dragged away.

"Good night to you both." Harold bowed over and the street was suddenly empty.

"That was close!" said Sam.

"Come a bit closer," I said.

It was a risk, but it was worth a try.

"How about a kiss?"

"Deal," smiled Sam.

So, not a bad night all round, really. Vampire sorted. And a girlfriend on my arm as we walked through the streets back home...

FOR TEACHERS

About

Freestylers is a series of carefully levelled stories, especially geared for struggling readers of both sexes. With very low reading age and high interest age, these books are humorous, fun, up-to-the-minute and edgy. Core characters provide familiarity in all of the stories, build confidence and ease pupils from one story through to the next, accelerating reading progress.

Freestylers can be used for both guided and independent reading. To make the most of the books you can:

• Focus on making each reading session successful. Talk about the text before the pupil starts reading. Introduce the characters, the storyline and any unfamiliar vocabulary.

• Encourage the pupil to talk about the book during reading and after reading. How would they have felt if they were Jas? Or Sam? How would they have gone about solving the mystery?

• Talk about which parts of the story they like best and why.

For guidance, this story has been approximately measured to:

National Curriculum Level: 2A　　　ATOS: 2.4
Reading Age: 6　　　Lexile ® Measure [confirmed]: 320L
Book Band: White